FRANK
O'CONNOR

THE GENIUS
AND OTHER STORIES

PENGUIN BOOKS

PENGUIN BOOKS

Published by the Penguin Group. Penguin Books Ltd, 27 Wrights Lane, London
w8 5TZ, England. Penguin Books USA Inc., 375 Hudson Street, New York, New
York 10014, USA. Penguin Books Australia Ltd, Ringwood, Victoria, Australia.
Penguin Books Canada Ltd., 10 Alcorn Avenue, Toronto, Ontario, Canada M4V 3B2.
Penguin Books (NZ) Ltd, 182–190 Wairau Road, Auckland 10, New Zealand ·
Penguin Books Ltd, Registered Offices: Harmondsworth, Middlesex, England ·
These four stories have been taken from *My Oedipus Complex and Other
Stories*, by Frank O'Connor, published by Penguin Books in 1963.
This edition published 1995 · Copyright © Frank O'Connor, 1953, 1957 ·
Typeset by Datix International Limited, Bungay, Suffolk · Printed in England by
Clays Ltd, St Ives plc · Except in the United States of America, this book is sold
subject to the condition that it shall not, by way of trade or otherwise, be lent, re-
sold, hired out, or otherwise circulated without the publisher's prior consent in any
form of binding or cover other than that in which it is published and without
a similar condition including this condition being imposed on the subsequent
purchaser · 10 9 8 7 6 5 4 3 2 1

CONTENTS

The Genius

I

Some kids are cissies by nature but I was a cissy by conviction. Mother had told me about geniuses; I wanted to be one, and I could see for myself that fighting, as well as being sinful, was dangerous. The kids round the Barrack where I lived were always fighting. Mother said they were savages, that I needed proper friends, and that once I was old enough to go to school I would meet them.

My way, when someone wanted to fight and I could not get away, was to climb on the nearest wall and argue like hell in a shrill voice about Our Blessed Lord and good manners. This was a way of attracting attention, and it usually worked because the enemy, having stared incredulously at me for several minutes, wondering if he would have time to hammer my head on the pavement before someone came out to him, yelled something like 'blooming cissy' and went away in disgust. I didn't like being called a cissy but I preferred it to fighting. I felt very like one of those poor mongrels who slunk through our neighbourhood and took to their heels when anyone came near them, and I always tried to make friends with them.

I toyed with games, and enjoyed kicking a ball gently before me along the pavement till I discovered that any boy who joined me grew violent and started to shoulder me out of the way. I preferred little girls because they didn't fight so much, but otherwise I found them insipid and lacking in any solid basis of information. The only women I cared for were grown-ups, and my most intimate friend was an old washer-woman called Miss Cooney who had been in the lunatic asylum and was very religious. It was she who had told me all about dogs. She would run a mile after anyone she saw hurting an animal, and even went to the police about them, but the police knew she was mad and paid no attention.

She was a sad-looking woman with grey hair, high cheekbones and toothless gums. While she ironed, I would sit for hours in the hot, steaming, damp kitchen, turning over the pages of her religious books. She was fond of me too, and told me she was sure I would be a priest. I agreed that I might be a bishop, but she didn't seem to think so highly of bishops. I told her there were so many other things I might be that I couldn't make up my mind, but she only smiled at this. Miss Cooney thought there was only one thing a genius could be and that was a priest.

On the whole I thought an explorer was what I would be. Our house was in a square between two roads, one terraced above the other, and I could leave home, follow the upper road for a mile past the Barrack, turn left on any of the intervening roads and lanes, and return almost without leaving the pavement. It was astonishing what valuable information you could pick up on a trip like that. When I came home I wrote down my adventures in a book called *The Voyages of Johnson Martin*, 'with many Maps and Illustrations, Irishtown University Press, 3s. 6d. nett'. I was also compiling *The Irishtown University Song Book for Use in Schools and Institutions by Johnson Martin*, which had the words and music of my favourite songs. I could not read music yet but I copied it from anything that came handy, preferring staff to solfa because it looked better on the page. But I still wasn't sure what I would be. All I knew was that I intended to be famous and have a statue put up to me near that of Father Matthew, in Patrick Street. Father Matthew was called the Apostle of Temperance, but I didn't think much of temperance. So far our town hadn't a proper genius and I intended to supply the deficiency.

3

But my work continued to bring home to me the great gaps in my knowledge. Mother understood my difficulty and worried herself endlessly finding answers to my questions, but neither she nor Miss Cooney had a great store of the sort of information I needed, and Father was more a hindrance than a help. He was talkative enough about subjects that interested himself but they did not greatly interest me. 'Ballybeg,' he would say brightly. 'Market town. Population 648. Nearest station, Rathkeale.' He was also forthcoming enough about other things, but later, Mother would take me aside and explain that he was only joking again. This made me mad, because I never knew when he was joking and when he wasn't.

I can see now, of course, that he didn't really like me. It was not the poor man's fault. He had never expected to be the father of a genius and it filled him with forebodings. He looked round him at all his contemporaries who had normal, bloodthirsty, illiterate children, and shuddered at the thought that I would never be good for anything but being a genius. To give him his due, it wasn't himself he worried about, but there had never been anything like it in the family before and he dreaded the shame of it. He would come in from the front door with his cap over his eyes and his hands in his trouser pockets and stare moodily at me while I sat at the kitchen table, surrounded by papers, producing fresh maps and illustrations for my book of voyages, or copying the music of 'The Minstrel Boy'.

'Why can't you go out and play with the Horgans?' he would ask wheedlingly, trying to make it sound attractive.

'I don't like the Horgans, Daddy,' I would reply politely.

'But what's wrong with them?' he would ask testily. 'They're fine manly young fellows.'

'They're always fighting, Daddy.'

'And what harm is fighting? Can't you fight them back?'

'I don't like fighting, Daddy, thank you,' I would say, still with perfect politeness.

'The dear knows, the child is right,' Mother would say, coming to my defence. 'I don't know what sort those children are.'

'Ah, you have him as bad as yourself,' Father would snort, and stalk to the front door again, to scald his heart with thoughts of the nice natural son he might have had if only he hadn't married the 5 wrong woman. Granny had always said Mother was the wrong woman for him and now she was being proved right.

She was being proved so right that the poor man couldn't keep his eyes off me, waiting for the insanity to break out in me. One of the things he didn't like was my Opera House. The Opera House was a cardboard box I had mounted on two chairs in the dark hallway. It had a proscenium cut in it, and I had painted some back-drops of mountain and sea, with wings that represented trees and rocks. The characters were pictures cut out, mounted and coloured, and moved on bits of stick. It was lit with candles, for which I had made coloured screens, greased so that they were transparent, and I made up operas from story-books and bits of songs. I was singing a passionate duet for two of the characters while twiddling the screens to produce the effect of moonlight when one of the screens caught fire and everything went up in a mass of flames. I screamed and Father came out to stamp out the blaze, and he cursed me till even Mother lost her temper with him and told him he was worse than six children, after which he wouldn't speak to her for a week.

6   Another time I was so impressed with a lame

teacher I knew that I decided to have a lame leg myself, and there was hell in the home for days because Mother had no difficulty at all in seeing that my foot was already out of shape while Father only looked at it and sniffed contemptuously. I was furious with him, and Mother decided he wasn't much better than a monster. They quarrelled for days over that until it became quite an embarrassment to me because, though I was bored stiff with limping, I felt I should be letting her down by getting better. When I went down the Square, lurching from side to side, Father stood at the gate, looking after me with a malicious knowing smile, and when I had discarded my limp, the way he mocked Mother was positively disgusting.

2

As I say, they squabbled endlessly about what I should be told. Father was for telling me nothing.

'But, Mick,' Mother would say earnestly, 'the child must learn.'

'He'll learn soon enough when he goes to school,' he snarled. 'Why do you be always at him, putting ideas into his head? Isn't he bad enough? I'd sooner the boy would grow up a bit natural.'

But either Mother didn't like children to be natural or she thought I was natural enough as I was. Women, of course, don't object to geniuses half as much as men do. I suppose they find them a relief.

Now one of the things I wanted badly to know was where babies came from, but this was something that no one seemed to be able to explain to me. When I asked Mother she got upset and talked about birds and flowers, and I decided that if she had ever known she must have forgotten it and was ashamed to say so. Miss Cooney only smiled wistfully when I asked her and said, 'You'll know all about it soon enough, child.'

'But, Miss Cooney,' I said with great dignity, 'I have to know now. It's for my work, you see.'

'Keep your innocence while you can, child,' she said in the same tone. 'Soon enough the world will rob you of it, and once 'tis gone 'tis gone for ever.'

But whatever the world wanted to rob me of, it was welcome to it from my point of view, if only I could get a few facts to work on. I appealed to Father and he told me that babies were dropped out 8 of aeroplanes and if you caught one you could keep it. 'By parachute?' I asked, but he only looked pained and said, 'Oh, no, you don't want to begin by spoiling them.' Afterwards, Mother took me aside again and explained that he was only joking. I went quite dotty with rage and told her that one of these days he would go too far with his jokes.

All the same, it was a great worry to Mother. It wasn't every mother who had a genius for a son, and she dreaded that she might be wronging me. She suggested timidly to Father that he should tell me something about it and he danced with rage. I heard them because I was supposed to be playing with the Opera House upstairs at the time. He said she was going out of her mind, and that she was driving me out of my mind at the same time. She was very upset because she had considerable respect for his judgement.

At the same time when it was a matter of duty she could be very, very obstinate. It was a heavy responsibility, and she disliked it intensely – a deeply pious woman who never mentioned the subject at all to anybody if she could avoid it – but it had to be done. She took an awful long time over it – it was a summer day, and we were sitting on the bank of a stream in the Glen – but at last I managed to detach the fact that mummies had an engine in their tummies and daddies had a starting-handle that made it work, and once it started it went on until it made a baby. That certainly explained an awful lot of things I had not understood up to this – for instance, why fathers were necessary and why Mother had buffers on her chest while Father had none. It made her almost as interesting as a locomotive, and for days I went round deploring my own rotten luck that I wasn't a girl and couldn't have an engine and buffers of my own instead of a measly old starting-handle like Father.

Soon afterwards I went to school and disliked it intensely. I was too small to be moved up to the big boys and the other 'infants' were still at the stage of spelling 'cat' and 'dog'. I tried to tell the old teacher about my work, but she only smiled and said, 'Hush, Larry!' I hated being told to hush. Father was always saying it to me.

One day I was standing at the playground gate, feeling very lonely and dissatisfied, when a tall girl from the Senior Girls' school spoke to me. She was a girl with a plump, dark face and black pigtails.

'What's your name, little boy?' she asked.

I told her.

'Is this your first time at school?' she asked.

'Yes.'

'And do you like it?'

'No, I hate it,' I replied gravely. 'The children can't spell and the old woman talks too much.'

Then I talked myself for a change and she listened attentively while I told her about myself, my voyages, my books and the time of the trains from all the city stations. As she seemed so interested I told her I would meet her after school and tell her some more.

I was as good as my word. When I had eaten my lunch, instead of going on further voyages I went back to the Girls' School and waited for her to come out. She seemed pleased to see me because she took my hand and brought me home with her. She lived up Gardiner's Hill, a steep, demure suburban road with trees that overhung the walls at either side. She lived in a small house on top of the hill and was one of a family of three girls. Her little brother, John Joe, had been killed the previous year by a car. 'Look at what I brought home with me!' she said when we went into the kitchen, and her mother, a tall, thin woman made a great fuss of me and wanted me to have my dinner with Una. That was the girl's name. I didn't take anything, but while she ate I sat by the range and told her mother about myself as well. She seemed to like it as much as Una, and when dinner was over Una took me out in the fields behind the house for a walk.

When I went home at teatime, Mother was delighted.

'Ah,' she said, 'I knew you wouldn't be long making nice friends at school. It's about time for you, the dear knows.'

I felt much the same about it, and every fine day at three I waited for Una outside the school. When it rained and Mother would not let me out I was miserable.

One day while I was waiting for her there were two senior girls outside the gate.

'Your girl isn't out yet, Larry,' said one with a giggle.

'And do you mean to tell me Larry has a girl?' the other asked with a shocked air.

'Oh, yes,' said the first. 'Una Dwyer is Larry's girl. He goes with Una, don't you, Larry?'

I replied politely that I did, but in fact I was seriously alarmed. I had not realized that Una would be considered my girl. It had never happened to me before, and I had not understood that my waiting for her would be regarded in such a grave light. Now, I think the girls were probably right anyhow, for that is always the way it has happened to me. A woman has only to shut up and let me talk long enough for me to fall head and ears in love with her. But then I did not recognize the symptoms. All I knew was that going with somebody meant you intended to marry them. I had always planned on marrying Mother; now it seemed as if I was expected to marry someone else, and I wasn't sure if I should like it or if, like football, it would prove to be one of those games that two people could not play without pushing.

A couple of weeks later I went to a party at Una's house. By this time it was almost as much mine as theirs. All the girls liked me and Mrs Dwyer talked to me by the hour. I saw nothing peculiar about this except a proper appreciation of geniuses. Una had warned me that I should be expected to sing, so I was ready for the occasion. I sang the Gregorian *Credo*, and some of the little girls laughed, but Mrs Dwyer only looked at me fondly.

'I suppose you'll be a priest when you grow up, Larry?' she asked.

'No, Mrs Dwyer,' I replied firmly. 'As a matter of fact, I intend to be a composer. Priests can't marry, you see, and I want to get married.'

That seemed to surprise her quite a bit. I was quite prepared to continue discussing my plans for the future, but all the children talked together. I was used to planning discussions so that they went on for a long time, but I found that whenever I began one in the Dwyers', it was immediately interrupted so that I found it hard to concentrate. Besides, all the children shouted, and Mrs Dwyer, for all her gentleness, shouted with them and at them. At first, I was somewhat alarmed, but I soon saw that they meant no particular harm, and when the party ended I was jumping up and down on the sofa, shrieking louder than anyone while Una, in hysterics of giggling, encouraged me. She seemed to think I was the funniest thing ever.

It was a moonlit November night, and lights were burning in the little cottages along the road when Una brought me home. On the road outside she stopped uncertainly and said, 'This is where little John Joe was killed.'

There was nothing remarkable about the spot, and I saw no chance of acquiring any useful information.

'Was it a Ford or a Morris?' I asked, more out of politeness than anything else.

14   'I don't know,' she replied with smouldering anger.

'It was Donegan's old car. They can never look where they're going, the old shows!'

'Our Lord probably wanted him,' I said perfunctorily.

'I dare say He did,' Una replied, though she showed no particular conviction. 'That old fool, Donegan – I could kill him whenever I think of it.'

'You should get your mother to make you another,' I suggested helpfully.

'Make me a what?' Una exclaimed in consternation.

'Make you another brother,' I repeated earnestly. 'It's quite easy, really. She has an engine in her tummy, and all your daddy has to do is to start it with his starting-handle.'

'Cripes!' Una said, and clapped her hand over her mouth in an explosion of giggles. 'Imagine me telling her that!'

'But it's true, Una,' I said obstinately. 'It only takes nine months. She could make you another little brother by next summer.'

'Oh, Jay!' exclaimed Una in another fit of giggles. 'Who told you all that?'

'Mummy did. Didn't your mother tell you?'

'Oh, she says you buy them from Nurse Daly,' said Una, and began to giggle again.

'I wouldn't really believe that,' I said with as much dignity as I could muster.

But the truth was I felt I had made a fool of myself again. I realized now that I had never been convinced by Mother's explanation. It was too simple. If there was anything that woman could get wrong she did so without fail. And it upset me, because for the first time I found myself wanting to make a really good impression. The Dwyers had managed to convince me that whatever else I wanted to be I did not want to be a priest. I didn't even want to be an explorer, a career which would take me away for long periods from my wife and family. I was prepared to be a composer and nothing but a composer.

That night in bed I sounded Mother on the subject of marriage. I tried to be tactful because it had always been agreed between us that I should marry her and I did not wish her to see that my feelings had changed.

'Mummy,' I asked, 'if a gentleman asks a lady to marry him, what does he say?'

'Oh,' she replied shortly, 'some of them say a lot. They say more than they mean.'

She was so irritable that I guessed she had divined my secret and I felt really sorry for her.

'If a gentleman said, "Excuse me, will you marry me?" would that be all right?' I persisted.

'Ah, well, he'd have to tell her first that he was fond of her,' said Mother who, no matter what she felt, could never bring herself to deceive me on any major issue.

But about the other matter I saw that it was hopeless to ask her any more. For days I made the most pertinacious inquiries at school and received some startling information. One boy had actually come floating down on a snowflake, wearing a bright blue dress, but to his chagrin and mine, the dress had been given away to a poor child in the North Main Street. I grieved long and deeply over this wanton destruction of evidence. The balance of opinion favoured Mrs Dwyer's solution, but of the theory of engines and starting-handles no one in the school had ever heard. That theory might have been all right when Mother was a girl but it was now definitely out of fashion.

And because of it I had been exposed to ridicule before the family whose good opinion I valued most. It was hard enough to keep up my dignity with a girl who was doing algebra while I hadn't got beyond long division without falling into childish errors that 17 made her laugh. That is another thing I still cannot stand, being made fun of by women. Once they begin on it they never stop. Once when we were going up Gardiner's Hill together after school she stopped to look at a baby in a pram. The baby grinned at her and she gave him her finger to suck. He waved his fists and sucked like mad, and she went off into giggles again.

'I suppose that was another engine?' she said.

Four times at least she mentioned my silliness, twice in front of other girls and each time, though I pretended to ignore it, I was pierced to the heart. It made me determined not to be exposed again. Once Mother asked Una and her younger sister, Joan, to tea, and all the time I was in an agony of self-consciousness, dreading what she would say next. I felt that a woman who had said such things about babies was capable of anything. Then the talk turned on the death of little John Joe, and it all flowed back into my mind on a wave of mortification. I made two efforts to change the conversation, but Mother returned to it. She was full of pity for the Dwyers, full of sympathy for the little boy and had almost reduced herself to tears. Finally I got up and ordered Una and Joan to play with me. Then Mother got angry.

'For goodness' sake, Larry, let the children finish their tea!' she snapped.

'It's all right, Mrs Delaney,' Una said good-naturedly. 'I'll go with him.'

'Nonsense, Una!' Mother said sharply. 'Finish your tea and go on with what you were saying. It's a wonder to me your poor mother didn't go out of her mind. How can they let people like that drive cars?'

At this I set up a loud wail. At any moment now I felt she was going to get on to babies and advise Una about what her mother ought to do.

'Will you behave yourself, Larry!' Mother said in a quivering voice. 'Or what's come over you in the past few weeks? You used to have such nice manners, and now look at you! A little corner boy! I'm ashamed of you!'

How could she know what had come over me? How could she realize that I was imagining the family circle in the Dwyers' house and Una, between fits of laughter, describing my old-fashioned mother who still talked about babies coming out of people's stomachs? It must have been real love, for I have never known true love in which I wasn't ashamed of Mother.

And she knew it and was hurt. I still enjoyed

going home with Una in the afternoons and while she ate her dinner, I sat at the piano and pretended to play my own compositions, but whenever she called at our house for me I grabbed her by the hand and tried to drag her away so that she and Mother shouldn't start talking.

'Ah, I'm disgusted with you,' Mother said one day. 'One would think you were ashamed of me in front of that little girl. I'll engage she doesn't treat her mother like that.'

Then one day I was waiting for Una at the school gate as usual. Another boy was waiting there as well – one of the seniors. When he heard the screams of the school breaking up he strolled away and stationed himself at the foot of the hill by the crossroads. Then Una herself came rushing out in her wide-brimmed felt hat, swinging her satchel, and approached me with a conspiratorial air.

'Oh, Larry, guess what's happened!' she whispered. 'I can't bring you home with me today. I'll come down and see you during the week though. Will that do?'

'Yes, thank you,' I said in a dead cold voice. Even at the most tragic moment of my life I could be nothing but polite. I watched her scamper down the hill to where the big boy was waiting. He looked over his shoulder with a grin, and then the two of them went off together.

Instead of following them I went back up the hill alone and stood leaning over the quarry wall, looking at the roadway and the valley of the city beneath me. I knew this was the end. I was too young to marry Una. I didn't know where babies came from and I didn't understand algebra. The fellow she had gone home with probably knew everything about both. I was full of gloom and revengeful thoughts. I, who had considered it sinful and dangerous to fight, was now regretting that I hadn't gone after him to batter his teeth in and jump on his face. It wouldn't even have mattered to me that I was too young and weak and that he would have done all the battering. I saw that love was a game that two people couldn't play at without pushing, just like football.

I went home and, without saying a word, took out the work I had been neglecting so long. That too seemed to have lost its appeal. Moodily I ruled five lines and began to trace the difficult sign of the treble clef.

'Didn't you see Una, Larry?' Mother asked in surprise, looking up from her sewing.

'No, Mummy,' I said, too full for speech.

'Wisha, 'twasn't a falling-out ye had?' she asked in dismay, coming towards me. I put my head on my hands and sobbed. 'Wisha, never mind, childeen!' she murmured, running her hand through my hair. 'She was a bit old for you. You reminded her of her little brother that was killed, of course – that was why. You'll soon make new friends, take my word for it.'

But I did not believe her. That evening there was no comfort for me. My great work meant nothing to me and I knew it was all I would ever have. For all the difference it made I might as well become a priest. I felt it was a poor, sad, lonesome thing being nothing but a genius.

My Oedipus Complex

Father was in the army all through the war – the First War, I mean – so, up to the age of five, I never saw much of him, and what I saw did not worry me. Sometimes I woke and there was a big figure in khaki peering down at me in the candlelight. Sometimes in the early morning I heard the slamming of the front door and the clatter of nailed boots down the cobbles of the lane. These were Father's entrances and exits. Like Santa Claus he came and went mysteriously.

In fact, I rather liked his visits, though it was an uncomfortable squeeze between Mother and him when I got into the big bed in the early morning. He smoked, which gave him a pleasant musty smell, and shaved, an operation of astounding interest. Each time he left a trail of souvenirs – model tanks and Gurkha knives with handles made of bullet cases, and German helmets and cap badges and buttonsticks, and all sorts of military equipment – carefully stowed away in a long box on top of the wardrobe, in case they ever came in handy. There was a bit of the magpie about Father; he expected everything to come in handy. When his back was turned, Mother let me get a chair and rummage through his treasures. She didn't seem to think so highly of them as he did.

The war was the most peaceful period of my life. The window of my attic faced south-east. My Mother had curtained it, but that had small effect. I always woke with the first light and, with all the responsibilities of the previous day melted, feeling myself rather like the sun, ready to illumine and rejoice. Life never seemed so simple and clear and full of possibilities as then. I put my feet out from under the clothes – I called them Mrs Left and Mrs Right – and invented dramatic situations for them in which they discussed the problems of the day. At least Mrs Right did; she was very demonstrative, but I hadn't the same control of Mrs Left, so she mostly contented herself with nodding agreement.

They discussed what Mother and I should do during the day, what Santa Claus should give a fellow for Christmas, and what steps should be taken to brighten the home. There was that little matter of the baby, for instance. Mother and I could never agree about that. Ours was the only house in the terrace without a new baby, and Mother said we couldn't afford one till Father came back from the war because they cost seventeen and six. That showed how simple she was. The Geneys up the road had a baby, and everyone knew they couldn't afford seventeen and six. It was probably a cheap baby, and Mother wanted something really good, but I felt she was too exclusive. The Geneys' baby would have done us fine.

Having settled my plans for the day, I got up, put a chair under the attic window, and lifted the frame high enough to stick out my head. The window overlooked the front gardens of the terrace behind ours, and beyond these it looked over a deep valley to the tall, red-brick houses terraced up the opposite hillside, which were all still in shadow, while those at our side of the valley were all lit up, though with long strange shadows that made them seem unfamiliar; rigid and painted.

After that I went into Mother's room and climbed into the big bed. She woke and I began to tell her of my schemes. By this time, though I never seem to have noticed it, I was petrified in my nightshirt, and I thawed as I talked until, the last frost melted, I fell asleep beside her and woke again only when I heard her below in the kitchen, making the breakfast.

After breakfast we went into town; heard Mass at St Augustine's and said a prayer for Father, and did the shopping. If the afternoon was fine we either went for a walk in the country or a visit to Mother's great friend in the convent, Mother St Dominic. Mother had them all praying for Father, and every night, going to bed, I asked God to send him back safe from the war to us. Little, indeed, did I know what I was praying for!

One morning I got into the big bed, and there, sure enough, was Father in his usual Santa Claus manner, but later, instead of uniform, he put on his best blue suit, and Mother was as pleased as anything. I saw nothing to be pleased about, because, out of uniform, Father was altogether less interesting, but she only beamed, and explained that our prayers had been answered, and off we went to Mass to thank God for having brought Father safely home.

The irony of it! That very day when he came in to dinner he took off his boots and put on his slippers, donned the dirty old cap he wore about the house to save him from colds, crossed his legs, and began to talk gravely to Mother, who looked anxious. Naturally, I disliked her looking anxious, because it destroyed her good looks, so I interrupted him.

'Just a moment, Larry!' she said gently.

This was only what she said when we had boring visitors, so I attached no importance to it and went on talking.

'Do be quiet, Larry!' she said impatiently. 'Don't you hear me talking to Daddy?'

This was the first time I had heard those ominous words, 'talking to Daddy', and I couldn't help feeling that if this was how God answered prayers, he couldn't listen to them very attentively.

'Why are you talking to Daddy?' I asked with as great a show of indifference as I could muster.

'Because Daddy and I have business to discuss. Now don't interrupt again!'

In the afternoon, at Mother's request, Father took me for a walk. This time we went into town instead of out to the country, and I thought at first, in my usual optimistic way, that it might be an improvement. It was nothing of the sort. Father and I had quite different notions of a walk in town. He had no proper interest in trams, ships, and horses, and the only thing that seemed to divert him was talking to fellows as old as himself. When I wanted to stop he simply went on, dragging me behind him by the hand; when he wanted to stop I had no alternative but to do the same. I noticed that it seemed to be a sign that he wanted to stop for a long time whenever he leaned against a wall. The second time I saw him do it I got wild. He seemed to be settling himself forever. I pulled him by the coat and trousers, but, unlike Mother who, if you were too persistent, got into a wax and said: 'Larry, if you don't behave yourself, I'll give you a good slap,' Father had an extraordinary capacity for amiable inattention. I sized him up and wondered would I cry, but he seemed to be too remote to be annoyed even by that. Really, it was like going for a walk with a mountain! He either ignored the wrenching and pummelling entirely, or else glanced down with a grin of amusement from his peak. I had never met anyone so absorbed in himself as he seemed.

At teatime, 'talking to Daddy' began again, complicated this time by the fact that he had an evening paper, and every few minutes he put it down and told Mother something new out of it. I felt this was foul play. Man for man, I was prepared to compete with him any time for Mother's attention, but when he had it all made up for him by other people it left me no chance. Several times I tried to change the
subject without success.

'You must be quiet while Daddy is reading, Larry,' Mother said impatiently.

It was clear that she either genuinely liked talking to Father better than talking to me, or else that he had some terrible hold on her which made her afraid to admit the truth.

'Mummy,' I said that night when she was tucking me up, 'do you think if I prayed hard God would send Daddy back to the war?'

She seemed to think about that for a moment.

'No, dear,' she said with a smile. 'I don't think he would.'

'Why wouldn't he, Mummy?'

'Because there isn't a war any longer, dear.'

'But, Mummy, couldn't God make another war, if He liked?'

'He wouldn't like to, dear. It's not God who makes wars, but bad people.'

'Oh!' I said.

I was disappointed about that. I began to think that God wasn't quite what he was cracked up to be.

Next morning I woke at my usual hour, feeling like a bottle of champagne. I put out my feet and invented a long conversation in which Mrs Right talked of the trouble she had with her own father till 29 she put him in the Home. I didn't quite know what the Home was but it sounded the right place for Father. Then I got my chair and stuck my head out of the attic window. Dawn was just breaking, with a guilty air that made me feel I had caught it in the act. My head bursting with stories and schemes, I stumbled in next door, and in the half-darkness scrambled into the big bed. There was no room at Mother's side so I had to get between her and Father. For the time being I had forgotten about him, and for several minutes I sat bolt-upright, racking my brains to know what I could do with him. He was taking up more than his fair share of the bed, and I couldn't get comfortable, so I gave him several kicks that made him grunt and stretch. He made room all right, though. Mother waked and felt for me. I settled back comfortably in the warmth of the bed with my thumb in my mouth.

'Mummy!' I hummed, loudly and contentedly.

'Sssh! dear,' she whispered. 'Don't wake Daddy!'

This was a new development, which threatened to be even more serious than 'talking to Daddy'. Life without my early-morning conferences was unthinkable.

'Why?' I asked severely.

'Because poor Daddy is tired.'

This seemed to me a quite inadequate reason, and I was sickened by the sentimentality of her 'poor Daddy'. I never liked that sort of gush; it always struck me as insincere.

'Oh!' I said lightly. Then in my most winning tone: 'Do you know where I want to go with you today, Mummy?'

'No, dear,' she sighed.

'I want to go down the Glen and fish for thorny-backs with my new net, and then I want to go out to the Fox and Hounds, and –'

'Don't-wake-Daddy!' she hissed angrily, clapping her hand across my mouth.

But it was too late. He was awake, or nearly so. He grunted and reached for the matches. Then he stared incredulously at his watch.

'Like a cup of tea, dear?' asked Mother in a meek, hushed voice I had never heard her use before. It sounded almost as though she were afraid.

'Tea?' he exclaimed indignantly. 'Do you know what the time is?'

'And after that I want to go up the Rathcooney Road,' I said loudly, afraid I'd forget something in all those interruptions.

31

'Go to sleep at once, Larry!' she said sharply.

I began to snivel. I couldn't concentrate, the way that pair went on, and smothering my early-morning schemes was like burying a family from the cradle.

Father said nothing, but lit his pipe and sucked it, looking out into the shadows without minding Mother or me. I knew he was mad. Every time I made a remark Mother hushed me irritably. I was mortified. I felt it wasn't fair; there was even something sinister in it. Every time I had pointed out to her the waste of making two beds when we could both sleep in one, she had told me it was healthier like that, and now here was this man, this stranger, sleeping with her without the least regard for her health!

He got up early and made tea, but though he brought Mother a cup he brought none for me.

'Mummy,' I shouted, 'I want a cup of tea, too.'

'Yes, dear,' she said patiently. 'You can drink from Mummy's saucer.'

That settled it. Either Father or I would have to leave the house. I didn't want to drink from Mother's saucer; I wanted to be treated as an equal in my own home, so, just to spite her, I drank it all and left none for her. She took that quietly, too.

But that night when she was putting me to bed she said gently:

'Larry, I want you to promise me something.'

'What is it?' I asked.

'Not to come in and disturb poor Daddy in the morning. Promise?'

'Poor Daddy' again! I was becoming suspicious of everything involving that quite impossible man.

'Why?' I asked.

'Because, poor Daddy is worried and tired and he doesn't sleep well.'

'Why doesn't he, Mummy?'

'Well, you know, don't you, that while he was at the war Mummy got the pennies from the Post Office?'

'From Miss MacCarthy?'

'That's right. But now, you see, Miss MacCarthy hasn't any more pennies, so Daddy must go out and find us some. You know what would happen if he couldn't?'

'No,' I said, 'tell us.'

'Well, I think we might have to go out and beg for them like the poor old woman on Fridays. We wouldn't like that, would we?'

'No,' I agreed. 'We wouldn't.'

'So you'll promise not to come in and wake him?'

'Promise.'

Mind you, I meant that. I knew pennies were a serious matter, and I was all against having to go out and beg like the old woman on Fridays. Mother laid out all my toys in a complete ring round the bed so that, whatever way I got out, I was bound to fall over one of them.

When I woke I remembered my promise all right. I got up and sat on the floor and played – for hours, it seemed to me. Then I got my chair and looked out the attic window for more hours. I wished it was time for Father to wake; I wished someone would make me a cup of tea. I didn't feel in the least like the sun; instead, I was bored and so very, very cold! I simply longed for the warmth and depth of the big featherbed.

At last I could stand it no longer. I went into the next room. As there was still no room at Mother's side I climbed over her and she woke with a start.

'Larry,' she whispered, gripping my arm very tightly, 'what did you promise?'

'But I did, Mummy,' I wailed, caught in the very act. 'I was quiet for ever so long.'

'Oh, dear, and you're perished!' she said sadly,

feeling me all over. 'Now, if I let you stay will you promise not to talk?'

'But I want to talk, Mummy,' I wailed.

'That has nothing to do with it,' she said with a firmness that was new to me. 'Daddy wants to sleep. Now, do you understand that?'

I understood it only too well. I wanted to talk, he wanted to sleep – whose house was it, anyway?

'Mummy,' I said with equal firmness, 'I think it would be healthier for Daddy to sleep in his own bed.'

That seemed to stagger her, because she said nothing for a while.

'Now, once for all,' she went on, 'you're to be perfectly quiet or go back to your own bed. Which is it to be?'

The injustice of it got me down. I had convicted her out of her own mouth of inconsistency and unreasonableness, and she hadn't even attempted to reply. Full of spite, I gave Father a kick, which she didn't notice but which made him grunt and open his eyes in alarm.

'What time is it?' he asked in a panic-stricken voice, not looking at Mother but at the door, as if he saw someone there.

'It's early yet,' she replied soothingly. 'It's only the child. Go to sleep again . . . Now, Larry,' she added, getting out of bed, 'you've wakened Daddy and you must go back.'

This time, for all her quiet air, I knew she meant it, and knew that my principal rights and privileges were as good as lost unless I asserted them at once. As she lifted me, I gave a screech, enough to wake the dead, not to mind Father. He groaned.

'That damn child! Doesn't he ever sleep?'

'It's only a habit, dear,' she said quietly, though I could see she was vexed.

'Well, it's time he got out of it,' shouted Father, beginning to heave in the bed. He suddenly gathered all the bedclothes about him, turned to the wall, and then looked back over his shoulder with nothing showing only two small, spiteful, dark eyes. The man looked very wicked.

To open the bedroom door, Mother had to let me down, and I broke free and dashed for the farthest corner, screeching. Father sat bolt upright in bed.

'Shut up, you little puppy!' he said in a choking voice.

I was so astonished that I stopped screeching. Never, never had anyone spoken to me in that tone before. I looked at him incredulously and saw his face convulsed with rage. It was only then that I fully realized how God had codded me, listening to my prayers for the safe return of this monster.

'Shut up, you!' I bawled, beside myself.

'What's that you said?' shouted Father, making a wild leap out of the bed.

'Mick, Mick!' cried Mother. 'Don't you see the child isn't used to you?'

'I see he's better fed than taught,' snarled Father, waving his arms wildly. 'He wants his bottom smacked.'

All his previous shouting was as nothing to these obscene words referring to my person. They really made my blood boil.

'Smack your own!' I screamed hysterically. 'Smack your own! Shut up! Shut up!'

At this he lost his patience and let fly at me. He did it with the lack of conviction you'd expect of a man under Mother's horrified eyes, and it ended up as a mere tap, but the sheer indignity of being struck at all by a stranger, a total stranger who had cajoled his way back from the war into our big bed as a result of my innocent intercession, made me completely dotty. I shrieked and shrieked, and danced in my bare feet, and Father, looking awkward and hairy in nothing but a short grey army shirt, glared down at me like a mountain out for murder. I think it must have been then that I realized he was jealous too. And there stood Mother in her nightdress, looking as if her heart was broken between us. I hoped she felt as she looked. It seemed to me that she deserved it all.

From that morning out my life was a hell. Father and I were enemies, open and avowed. We conducted a series of skirmishes against one another, he trying to steal my time with Mother and I his. When she was sitting on my bed, telling me a story, he took to looking for some pair of old boots which he alleged he had left behind him at the beginning of the war. While he talked to Mother I played loudly with my toys to show my total lack of concern. He created a terrible scene one evening when he came in from work and found me at his box, playing with his regimental badges, Gurkha knives, and button-sticks. Mother got up and took the box from me.

'You mustn't play with Daddy's toys unless he lets you, Larry,' she said severely. 'Daddy doesn't play with yours.'

For some reason Father looked at her as if she had struck him and then turned away with a scowl.

'Those are not toys,' he growled, taking down the box again to see had I lifted anything. 'Some of those curios are very rare and valuable.'

But as time went on I saw more and more how he managed to alienate Mother and me. What made it worse was that I couldn't grasp his method or see what attraction he had for Mother. In every possible way he was less winning than I. He had a common accent and made noises at his tea. I thought for a while that it might be the newspapers she was interested in, so I made up bits of news of my own to read to her. Then I thought it might be the smoking, which I personally thought attractive, and took his pipes and went round the house dribbling into them till he caught me. I even made noises at my tea, but Mother only told me I was disgusting. It all seemed to hinge round that unhealthy habit of sleeping together, so I made a point of dropping into their bedroom and nosing round, talking to myself, so that they wouldn't know I was watching them, but they were never up to anything that I could see. In the end it beat me. It seemed to depend on being grown-up and giving people rings, and I realized I'd have to wait.

But at the same time I wanted him to see that I

was only waiting, not giving up the fight. One evening when he was being particularly obnoxious, chattering away well above my head, I let him have it.

'Mummy,' I said, 'do you know what I'm going to do when I grow up?'

'No, dear,' she replied. 'What?'

'I'm going to marry you,' I said quietly.

Father gave a great guffaw out of him, but he didn't take me in. I knew it must only be pretence. And Mother, in spite of everything, was pleased. I felt she was probably relieved to know that one day Father's hold on her would be broken.

'Won't that be nice?' she said with a smile.

'It'll be very nice,' I said confidently. 'Because we're going to have lots and lots of babies.'

'That's right, dear,' she said placidly. 'I think we'll have one soon, and then you'll have plenty of company.'

I was no end pleased about that because it showed that in spite of the way she gave in to Father she still considered my wishes. Besides, it would put the Geneys in their place.

It didn't turn out like that, though. To begin with, she was very preoccupied – I supposed about where she would get the seventeen and six – and though Father took to staying out late in the evenings it did me no particular good. She stopped taking me for walks, became as touchy as blazes, and smacked me for nothing at all. Sometimes I wished I'd never mentioned the confounded baby – I seemed to have a genius for bringing calamity on myself.

And calamity it was! Sonny arrived in the most appalling hullabaloo – even that much he couldn't do without a fuss – and from the first moment I disliked him. He was a difficult child – so far as I was concerned he was always difficult – and demanded far too much attention. Mother was simply silly about him, and couldn't see when he was only showing off. As company he was worse than useless. He slept all day, and I had to go round the house on tiptoe to avoid waking him. It wasn't any longer a question of not waking Father. The slogan now was 'Don't-wake-Sonny!' I couldn't understand why the child wouldn't sleep at the proper time, so whenever Mother's back was turned I woke him. Sometimes to keep him awake I pinched him as well. Mother caught me at it one day and gave me a most unmerciful flaking.

One evening, when Father was coming in from

work, I was playing trains in the front garden. I let on not to notice him; instead, I pretended to be talking to myself, and said in a loud voice: 'If another bloody baby comes into this house, I'm going out.'

Father stopped dead and looked at me over his shoulder.

'What's that you said?' he asked sternly.

'I was only talking to myself,' I replied, trying to conceal my panic. 'It's private.'

He turned and went in without a word. Mind you, I intended it as a solemn warning, but its effect was quite different. Father started being quite nice to me. I could understand that, of course. Mother was quite sickening about Sonny. Even at mealtimes she'd get up and gawk at him in the cradle with an idiotic smile, and tell Father to do the same. He was always polite about it, but he looked so puzzled you could see he didn't know what she was talking about. He complained of the way Sonny cried at night, but she only got cross and said that Sonny never cried except when there was something up with him – which was a flaming lie, because Sonny never had anything up with him, and only cried for attention. It was really painful to see how simple-minded she was. Father wasn't attractive, but he had a fine intelligence. He saw through Sonny, and now he knew that I saw through him as well.

One night I woke with a start. There was someone beside me in the bed. For one wild moment I felt sure it must be Mother, having come to her senses and left Father for good, but then I heard Sonny in convulsions in the next room, and Mother saying: 'There! There! There!' and I knew it wasn't she. It was Father. He was lying beside me, wide awake, breathing hard and apparently as mad as hell.

After a while it came to me what he was mad about. It was his turn now. After turning me out of the big bed, he had been turned out himself. Mother had no consideration now for anyone but that poisonous pup, Sonny. I couldn't help feeling sorry for Father. I had been through it all myself, and even at that age I was magnanimous. I began to stroke him down and say: 'There! There!' He wasn't exactly responsive.

'Aren't you asleep either?' he snarled.

'Ah, come on and put your arm around us, can't you?' I said, and he did, in a sort of way. Gingerly, I suppose, is how you'd describe it. He was very bony but better than nothing.

At Christmas he went out of his way to buy me a really nice model railway.

The Ugly Duckling

I

Mick Courtney had known Nan Ryan from the time he was fourteen or fifteen. She was the sister of his best friend, and youngest of a family of four in which she was the only girl. He came to be almost as fond of her as her father and brothers were; she had practically lost her mother's regard by inheriting her father's looks. Her ugliness indeed was quite endearing. She had a stocky, sturdy figure and masculine features all crammed into a feminine container till it bulged. None of her features was really bad, and her big, brown, twinkling eyes were delightful, but they made a group that was almost comic.

Her brothers liked her spirit; they let her play with them while any of them was of an age for play, and, though she suffered from night-panics and Dinny broke the maternal rule by letting her into his bed, they never told. He, poor kid, would be wakened in the middle of the night by Nan's pulling and shaking. 'Dinny, Dinny,' she would hiss fiercely, 'I have 'em again!' 'What are they this time?' Dinny would ask drowsily. 'Li-i-ons!' she would reply in a blood-curdling tone, and then lie for half an hour in his arms, contracting her toes and kicking spasmodically while he patted and soothed her.

She grew up a tomboy, fierce, tough, and tearless, fighting in Dinny's gang, which contested the old quarry on the road with the hill-tribes from the slum area above it; and this was how Mick was to remember her best; an ugly, stocky little Amazon, leaping from rock to rock, hurling stones in an awkward but effective way and screaming deadly insults at the enemy and encouragement to her own side.

He could not have said when she gave up fighting, but between twelve and fourteen she became the pious one in a family not remarkable for piety; always out at Mass or diving into church on her way from school to light candles and make novenas. Afterwards it struck Mick that it might have been an alternative to getting in Dinny's bed, for she still suffered from night-fears, only now when they came on she grabbed her rosary beads instead.

It amused him to discover that she had developed something of a crush on himself. Mick had lost his faith, which in Cork is rather similar to a girl's loss of her virtue and starts the same sort of flutterings among the quiet ones of the opposite sex. Nan would be waiting for him at the door in the evening, and when she saw him would begin to jump down the steps one by one with her feet together, her hands stiff at her sides, and her pigtail tossing.

'How are the novenas coming on, Nan?' he would ask with amusement.

'Fine!' she would reply in a shrill, expressionless voice. 'You're on your way.'

'I'll come quietly.'

'You think you won't, but I know better. I'm a fierce pray-er.'

Another stiff jump took her past him.

'Why don't you do it for the blacks, Nan?'

'I'm doing it for them too, sure.'

But though her brothers could ease the pangs of childhood for her, adolescence threw her on the mercy of life. Her mother, a roly-poly of a woman who went round a great deal with folded arms, thus increasing the impression of curves and rolls, was still a beauty, and did her best to disguise Nan's ugliness, a process that mystified her husband who could see nothing lacking in the child except her shaky mathematics.

46   'I'm no blooming beauty,' Nan would cry with an

imitation of a schoolboy's toughness whenever her mother tried to get her out of the rough tweeds and dirty pullovers she fancied into something more feminine.

'The dear knows you're not,' her mother would say, folding her arms with an expression of resignation. 'I don't suppose you want to advertise it though.'

'Why wouldn't I advertise it?' Nan would cry, squaring up to her. 'I don't want any of your dirty old men.'

'You needn't worry, child. They'll let you well alone.'

'Let them!' Nan would say, scowling. 'I don't care. I want to be a nun.'

All the same it made her self-conscious about friendships with girls of her own age, even pious ones like herself. They too would have boys around, and the boys wanted nothing to do with Nan. Though she carefully avoided all occasion for a slight, even the hint of one was enough to make her brooding and resentful, and then she seemed to become hideous and shapeless and furtive. She slunk round the house with her shoulders up about her ears, her red-brown hair hanging loose and a cigarette glued loosely to her lower lip. Suddenly and inexplicably she would drop some quite nice girl she had been friendly with for years and never even speak of her again. It gave her the reputation of being cold and insincere, but as Dinny in his shrewd, old-mannish way observed to Mick, she made her real friends among older women and even sick people – 'all seventy or paralysed' as he put it. Yet, even with these she tended to be jealous and exacting.

Dinny didn't like this, and his mother thought it was awful, but Nan paid no attention to their views. She had become exceedingly obstinate in a way that did not suit either her age or her sex, and it made her seem curiously angular, almost masculine, as though it were the psychological aspect of her ugliness. She had no apparent shyness and stalked in and out of a room, swinging her arms like a boy. Her conversation changed too, and took on the tone of an older woman's. It was not dull – she was far too brainy to be dull – but it was too much on one key – 'crabbed' to use a local word – and it did not make the sharp distinctions young people's conversation makes between passion and boredom. Dinny and Mick could be very bored indeed in one another's company, but suddenly some topic would set flame to their minds, and they would walk the streets by the hour with their coats buttoned up, arguing.

Her father was disappointed when she refused to go to college. When she did go to work it was in a dress shop, a curious occupation for a girl whose only notions of dress were a trousers and jersey.

2

Then one night something happened that electrified Mick. It was more like a transformation scene in a pantomime than anything in his experience. Later, of course, he realized that it had not happened like that at all. It was just that, as usual with those one has known too well, he had ceased to observe Nan, had taken her too much for granted, and the change in her had come about gradually and imperceptibly till it forced itself on his attention in the form of a shock.

Dinny was upstairs and Mick and she were arguing. Though without formal education, Mick was a well-read man, and he had no patience with Nan's literary tastes which were those of her aged and invalid acquaintances – popular novels and biographies.

As usual he made fun of her and as usual she grew angry. 'You're so damn superior, Mick Courtney,' she said with a scowl and went to search for the book they had discussed in the big mahogany bookcase, which was one of the handsome pieces of furniture her mother took pride in. Laughing, Mick got up and stood beside her, putting his arm round her shoulder as he would have done at any other time. She misunderstood the gesture for she leaned back on his shoulder and offered herself to be kissed. At that moment only did he realize that she had turned into a girl of startling beauty. He did not kiss her. Instead, he dropped his arm and looked at her incredulously. She gave him a malicious grin and went on with her search.

For the rest of the evening he could not take his eyes from her. Now he could easily analyse the change for himself. He remembered that she had been ill with some type of fever and had come out of it white and thin. Then she had seemed to shoot up, and now he saw that during her illness her face had lengthened and one by one each of those awkward lumps of feature had dropped into place and proportion till they formed a perfect structure that neither 50 age nor illness could any longer quite destroy. It was not in the least like her mother's type of beauty which was round and soft and eminently pattable. It was like a translation of her father's masculinity, tight and strained and almost harsh, and she had deliberately emphasized it by the way she pulled her hair back in a tight knot, exposing the rather big ears. Already it had begun to affect her gait because she no longer charged about a room, swinging her arms like a sergeant-major. At the same time she had not yet learned to move gracefully, and she seemed to drift rather than walk, and came in and went out in profile as though afraid to face a visitor or turn her back on him. And he wondered again at the power of habit that causes us to live with people historically, with faults or virtues that have long disappeared to every eye but our own.

For twelve months Mick had been going steadily with a nice girl from Sunday's Well and in due course he would have married her. Mick was that sort; a creature of habit who controlled circumstances by simplifying them down to a routine – the same restaurant, the same table, the same waitress, and the same dish. It enabled him to go on with his own thoughts. But whenever anything did happen to disturb this routine it was like a convulsion of Nature for him; even his favourite restaurant became a burden and he did not know what to do with his evenings and week-ends. The transformation of Nan into a beauty had a similar effect on him. Gradually he dropped the nice girl from Sunday's Well without a word of explanation or apology and went more and more to the Ryans, where he had a feeling of not being particularly welcome to anyone but Dinny and – sometimes at least – to Nan herself.

She had plenty of admirers without him. Mr Ryan, a tall, bald, noisy man with an ape-like countenance of striking good nature, enjoyed it as proof that sensible men were not put off by a girl's mathematics – he, poor man, had noticed no change whatever in his daughter. Mrs Ryan had no such pleasure. Naturally, she had always cared more for her sons, but they had not brought home with them attractive young men who were compelled to flirt with her, and now Nan took an almost perverse delight in keeping the young men and her mother apart. Beauty had brought out what ugliness had failed to do – a deep resentment of her mother that at times went too far for Mick's taste. Occasionally he saw it in a reversion to a heavy, stolid, almost stupid air that harked back to her childhood, sometimes in a sparkle of wit that had malice in it. She made up for this by what Mick thought of as an undue consideration for her father. Whenever he came into the room, bellowing and cheerful, her face lit up.

She had ceased to wear the rough masculine tweeds she had always preferred and to Mick's eye it was not a change for the better. She had developed a passion for good clothes without an understanding of them, and she used powder and lipstick in the lavish tasteless manner of a girl of twelve.

But if he disapproved of her taste in dress, he hated her taste in men. What left Dinny bored made Mick mad. He and Nan argued about this in the same way they argued about books. 'Smoothies,' he called her admirers to her face. There was Joe Lyons, the solicitor, a suave, dark-haired young man with mysterious slit-like eyes who combined a knowledge of wines with an intellectual Catholicism, and Matt Healy, a little leprechaun of a butter merchant who had a boat and rattled on cheerfully about whisky and 'dames'. The pair of them could argue for a full half-hour about a particular make of car or a Dublin hotel without, so far as Mick could see, ever uttering one word of sense, and obviously Lyons despised 53

Healy as a chatter-box and Healy despised Lyons as a fake, while both of them despised Mick. They thought he was a character, and whenever he tried to discuss religion or politics with them they listened with an amusement that made him furious.

'I stick to Mick against the day the Revolution comes,' said Healy with his leprechaun's laugh.

'No,' Lyons said, putting his arm patronizingly about Mick, 'Mick will have nothing to do with revolutions.'

'Don't be too sure,' said Healy, his face lit up with merriment. 'Mick is a *sans-culotte*. Isn't that the word, Mick?'

'I repeat no,' said Lyons with his grave smile. 'I know Mick. Mick is a wise man. Mind,' he added solemnly, raising his finger, 'I didn't say an intelligent man. I said a wise one. There's a difference.'

Mick could not help being angry. When they talked that way to Dinny he only blinked politely and drifted upstairs to his book or his gramophone, but Mick stayed and grew mad. He was hard-working but unambitious; too intelligent to value the things commonplace people valued, but too thin-skinned to ignore their scorn at his failure to do so.

54   Nan herself had no objection to being courted by

Mick. She was still under the influence of her childish infatuation, and it satisfied her vanity to be able to indulge it. She was an excellent companion, active and intelligent, and would go off for long walks with him over the hills through the fields to the river. They would end up in a public house in Glanmire or Little Island, though she soon stopped him trying to be extravagant in the manner of Lyons and Healy. 'I'm a whisky drinker, Mick,' she would say with a laugh. 'You're not a whisky buyer.' She could talk for an hour over a glass of beer, but when Mick tried to give their conversation a sentimental turn she countered with a bluff practicality that shocked him.

'Marry you?' she exclaimed with a laugh. 'Who died and left you the fortune?'

'Why, do I have to have a fortune?' he asked quietly, though he was stung by her good-natured contempt.

'Well, it would be a help if you're thinking of getting married,' she replied with a laugh. 'As long as I remember my family, we never seem to have been worried by anything else.'

'Of course, if you married Joe Lyons, you wouldn't have to worry,' he said with a hint of a sneer.

'From my point of view, that would be a very good reason,' she said.

'A classy car and St Thomas Aquinas,' Mick went on, feeling like a small boy but unable to stop himself. 'What more could a girl ask?'

'You resent people having cars, don't you?' she asked, leaning her elbows on the table and giving him a nasty look. 'Don't you think it might help if you went and got one for yourself?'

The worldly, middle-aged tone, particularly when linked with the Ryan go-getting, could be exceedingly destructive. There was something else that troubled him, too, though he was not sure why. He had always liked to pose a little as a man of the world, but Nan could sometimes shock him badly. There seemed to be depths of sensuality in her that were out of character. He could not believe that she really intended it, but she could sometimes inflame him with some sudden violence or coarseness as no ordinary girl could do.

Then one evening when they were out together, walking in the Lee Fields, he noticed a change in her. She and another girl had been spending a few days in Glengarriffe with Lyons and Healy. She did not want to talk of it, and he had the feeling that something about it had disappointed her. She was

 different; brooding, affectionate, and intense. She

pulled off her shoes and stockings and sat with her feet in the river, her hands joined between her knees while she gazed at the woods on the other side of the river.

'You think too much of Matt and Joe,' she said, splashing her feet. 'Why can't you feel sorry for them?'

'Feel sorry for them?' he repeated, so astonished that he burst into a laugh. She turned her head and her brown eyes rested on him with a strange innocence.

'If you weren't such an old agnostic, I'd say pray for them.'

'For what?' he asked, still laughing. 'Bigger dividends?'

'The dividends aren't much use to them,' she said. 'They're both bored. That's why they like me – I don't bore them. They don't know what to make of me . . . Mind,' she added, laughing in her enthusiastic way, 'I love money, Mick Courtney. I love expensive clothes and flashy dinners and wines I can't pronounce the names of, but they don't take me in. A girl who was brought up as I was needs more than that to take her in.'

'What is it you need?' asked Mick.

'Why don't you go and do something?' she asked with sudden gravity.

'What?' he replied with a shrug.

'What?' she asked, waving her hands. 'What do I care? I don't even know what you care about. I don't mind if you make a mess of it. It's not failure I'm afraid of. It's just getting stuck in the mud, not caring for anything. Look at Daddy! You may not think so, but I know he's a brilliant man, and he's stuck. Now he hopes the boys will find out whatever secret there is and do all the things he couldn't do. That doesn't appeal to me.'

'Yes,' Mick agreed thoughtfully, lighting a cigarette and answering himself rather than her. 'I know what you mean. I dare say I'm not ambitious. I've never felt the need for being ambitious. But I fancy I could be ambitious for someone else. I'd have to get out of Cork though. Probably to Dublin. There's nothing here in my line.'

'Dublin would do me fine,' she said with satisfaction. 'Mother and I would get on much better at that distance.'

He said nothing for a few moments, and Nan went on splashing gaily with her feet.

'Is that a bargain then?' he asked.

'Oh, ycs,' she said, turning her big soft eyes on him. 'That's a bargain. Don't you know I was always mad about you?'

Their engagement made a big change in Mick. He was, as I have said, a creature of habit, a man who lived by associations. He really knew the city in a way that few of us knew it, its interesting corners and queer characters, and the idea of having to exchange it for a place of no associations at all was more of a shock to him than it would have been to any of us; but though at certain times it left him with a lost feeling, at others it restored to him a boyish excitement and gaiety as though the trip he was preparing for was some dangerous voyage from which he might not return, and when he lit up like that he became more attractive, reckless, and innocent. Nan had always been attracted by him; now she really admired and loved him.

All the same she did not discontinue her outings with her other beaux. In particular, she remained friendly with Lyons, who was really fond of her and believed that she wasn't serious about marrying Mick. He was, as she said, a genuinely kind man, and was shocked at the thought that so beautiful a girl should even consider cooking and washing clothes on a clerk's income. He went to her father about it, and explained patiently to him that it would mean social extinction for Nan, and would even have gone to Mick himself but that Nan forbade it. 'But he can't do it, Nan,' he protested earnestly. 'Mick is a decent man. He can't do that to you.' 'He can't like hell,' said Nan, chuckling and putting her head on Lyons's chest. 'He'd send me out on the streets to keep himself in fags.'

These minor infidelities did not in the least worry Mick, who was almost devoid of jealousy. He was merely amused by her occasional lies and evasions and even more by the fits of conscience that followed them.

'Mick,' she asked between anger and laughter, 'why do I tell you all these lies? I'm not naturally untruthful, am I? I didn't go to confession on Saturday night. I went out with Joe Lyons instead. He still believes I'm going to marry him, and I would, too, if only he had a brain in his head. Mick, why can't you be attractive like that?'

But if Mick didn't resent it, Mrs Ryan resented it on his behalf, though she resented his complaisance even more. She was sufficiently feminine to know she might have done the same herself, and to feel that if she had, she would need correction. No man is ever as anti-feminist as a really feminine woman.

No, it was Nan's father who exasperated Mick, and he was sensible enough to realize that he was being exasperated without proper cause. When Joe Lyons lamented Nan's decision to Tom Ryan as though it were no better than suicide, the old man was thunderstruck. He had never mixed in society himself which might be the reason that he had never got anywhere in life.

'You really think it would come to that, Joe?' he asked, scowling.

'But consider it for yourself, Mr Ryan,' pleaded Joe, raising that warning finger of his. 'Who is going to receive them? They can always come to my house, but I'm not everybody. Do you think they'll be invited to the Healys? I say, the moment they marry, Matt will drop them, and I won't blame him. It's a game, admitted, but you have to play it. Even I have to play it, and my only interest is in philosophy.'

By the end of the evening Tom Ryan had managed to persuade himself that Mick was almost a ne'er-do-well and certainly an adventurer. The prospect of the Dublin job did not satisfy him in the least. He wanted to know what Mick proposed to do then.

Rest on his oars? There were examinations he could take which would ensure his chances of promotion. Tom would arrange it all and coach him himself.

At first Mick was amused and patient; then he became sarcastic, a great weakness of his whenever he was forced on the defensive. Tom Ryan, who was as incapable as a child of understanding sarcasm, rubbed his bald head angrily and left the room in a flurry. If Mick had only hit him over the head, as his wife did whenever he got on her nerves, Tom would have understood that he was only relieving his feelings, and liked him the better for it. But sarcasm was to him a sort of silence, a denial of attention that hurt him bitterly.

'I wish you wouldn't speak to Daddy like that,' Nan said one night when her father had been buzzing about Mick with syllabuses he had refused even to look at.

'I wish Daddy would stop arranging my life for me,' Mick said wearily.

'He only means it in kindness.'

'I didn't think he meant it any other way,' Mick said stiffly. 'But I wish he'd get it into his head that I'm marrying you, not him.'

'I wouldn't be too sure of that either, Mick,' she said angrily.

'Really, Nan!' he said reproachfully. 'Do you want me to be pushed round by your old man?'

'It's not only that,' she said, rising and crossing the room to the fireplace. He noticed that when she lost her temper, she suddenly seemed to lose command of her beauty. She scowled, bowed her head, and walked with a heavy guardsman's tread. 'It's just as well we've had this out, because I'd have had to tell you anyway. I've thought about it enough, God knows. I can't possibly marry you.'

Her tone was all that was necessary to bring Mick back to his own tolerant, reasonable self.

'Why not?' he asked gently.

'Because I'm scared, if you want to know.' And just then, looking down at him, she seemed scared.

'Of marriage?'

'Of marriage as well.' He noticed the reservation.

'Of me, so?'

'Oh, of marriage and you and myself,' she said explosively. 'Myself most of all.'

'Afraid you may kick over the traces?' he asked with affectionate mockery.

'You think I wouldn't?' she hissed, with clenched fists, her eyes narrowing and her face looking old and grim. 'You don't understand me at all, Mick 63

Courtney,' she added, with a sort of boyish braggadocio that made her seem again like the little tomboy he had known. 'You don't even know the sort of things I'm capable of. You're wrong for me. I always knew you were.'

Mick treated the scene lightly as though it were merely another of their disagreements, but when he left the house he was both hurt and troubled. Clearly there was a side of her character that he did not understand, and he was a man who liked to understand things, if only so that he could forget about them and go on with his own thoughts. Even on the familiar hill-street with the gas-lamp poised against the night sky, he seemed to be walking a road without associations. He knew Nan was unhappy and felt it had nothing to do with the subject of their quarrel. It was unhappiness that had driven her into his arms in the first place, and now it was as though she were being driven out again by the same wind. He had assumed rather too complacently that she had turned to him in the first place because she had seen through Lyons and Healy, but now he felt that her unhappiness had nothing to do with them either. She was desperate about herself rather than them. It struck him that she might easily have been tempted too far by Lyons's good looks and kindness. She was the sort of passionate girl who could very easily be lured into an indiscretion and who would then react from it in loathing and self-disgust. The very thought that this might be the cause moved him to a passion of protective tenderness, and before he went to bed he wrote and posted an affectionate letter, apologizing for his rudeness to her father and promising to consider her feelings more in the future.

In reply, he got a brief note, delivered at his house while he was at work. She did not refer at all to his letter, and told him that she was marrying Lyons. It was a dry note, and, for him, full of suppressed malice. He left his own house and met Dinny on the way up to call for him. From Dinny's gloomy air Mick saw that he knew all about it. They went for one of their usual country walks, and only when they were sitting in a country pub over their beer did Mick speak of the breach.

Dinny was worried and his worry made him rude, and through the rudeness Mick seemed to hear the voices of the Ryans discussing him. They hadn't really thought much of him as a husband for Nan but had been prepared to put up with him on her account. At the same time there was no question in their minds but that she didn't really care for Lyons and was marrying him only in some mood of desperation induced by Mick. Obviously, it was all Mick's fault.

'I can't really imagine what I did,' Mick said reasonably. 'Your father started bossing me and I was rude to him. I know that, and I told Nan I was sorry.'

'Oh, the old man bosses us all, and we're all rude,' said Dinny. 'It's not that.'

'Then it's nothing to do with me,' Mick said doggedly.

'Maybe not,' replied Dinny without conviction. 'But whatever it is, the harm is done. You know how obstinate Nan is when she takes an idea into her head.'

'And you don't think I should see her and ask her?'

'I wouldn't,' said Dinny, looking at Mick directly for the first time. 'I don't think Nan will marry you, old man, and I'm not at all sure but that it might be the best thing for you. You know I'm fond of her but she's a curious girl. I think you'll only hurt

yourself worse than you're hurt already.'

Mick realized that Dinny, for whatever reasons, was advising him to quit, and for once he was in a position to do so. With the usual irony of events, the job in Dublin he had been seeking only on her account had been offered to him, and he would have to leave at the end of the month.

This, which had seemed an enormous break with his past, now turned out to be the very best solace for his troubled mind. Though he missed old friends and familiar places more than most people, he had the sensitiveness of his type to any sort of novelty, and soon ended by wondering how he could ever have stuck Cork for so long. Within twelve months he had met a nice girl called Eilish and married her. And though Cork people might be parochial, Eilish believed that anything that didn't happen between Glasnevin and Terenure had not happened at all. When he talked to her of Cork her eyes simply glazed over.

So entirely did Cork scenes and characters fade from his memory that it came as a shock to him to meet Dinny one fine day in Grafton Street. Dinny was on his way to his first job in England, and Mick at once invited him home. But before they left town they celebrated their reunion in Mick's favourite pub off Grafton Street. Then he could ask the question that had sprung to his mind when he caught sight of Dinny's face.

'How's Nan?'

'Oh, didn't you hear about her?' Dinny asked with his usual air of mild surprise. 'Nan's gone into a convent, you know.'

'Nan?' repeated Mick. 'Into a convent?'

'Yes,' said Dinny. 'Of course, she used to talk of it when she was a kid, but we never paid much attention. It came as a surprise to us. I fancy it surprised the convent even more,' he added dryly.

'For God's sake!' exclaimed Mick. 'And the fellow she was engaged to – Lyons?'

'Oh, she dropped him inside a couple of months,' said Dinny with distaste. 'I never thought she was serious about him anyway. The fellow is a damned idiot.'

Mick went on with his drink, suddenly feeling embarrassed and strained. A few minutes later he asked with the pretence of a smile:

'You don't think if I'd hung on she might have changed her mind?'

'I dare say she might,' Dinny replied sagaciously.

'I'm not so sure it would have been the best thing

for you though,' he added kindly. 'The truth is, I don't think Nan is the marrying kind.'

'I dare say not,' said Mick, but he did not believe it for an instant. He was quite sure that Nan was the marrying kind, and that nothing except the deep unhappiness that had first united and then divided them had kept her from marrying. But what that unhappiness was about he still had no idea, and he saw that Dinny knew even less than he did.

Their meeting had brought it all back, and at intervals during the next few years it returned again to his mind, disturbing him. It was not that he was unhappy in his own married life – a man would have to have something gravely wrong with him to be unhappy with a girl like Eilish – but sometimes in the morning when he kissed her at the gate and went swinging down the ugly modern avenue towards the sea, he would think of the river or the hills of Cork and of the girl who had seemed to have none of his pleasure in simple things, whose decisions seemed all to have been dictated by some inner torment.

Then, long after, he found himself alone in Cork, tidying up things after the death of his father, his last relative there, and was suddenly plunged back into the world of his childhood and youth, wandering like a ghost from street to street, from pub to pub, from old friend to old friend, resurrecting other ghosts in a mood that was half anguish, half delight. He walked out to Blackpool and up Goulding's Glen only to find that the big mill-pond had all dried up, and sat on the edge remembering winter days when he was a child and the pond was full of skaters, and summer nights when it was full of stars. His absorption in the familiar made him peculiarly susceptible to the poetry of change. He visited the Ryans and found Mrs Ryan almost as good-looking and pattable as ever, though she moaned sentimentally about the departure of the boys, her disappointment with Nan and her husband's growing crankiness.

When she saw him to the door she folded her arms and leaned against the jamb.

'Wisha, Mick, wouldn't you go and see her?' she asked reproachfully.

'Nan?' said Mick. 'You don't think she'd mind?'

'Why would she mind, boy?' Mrs Ryan said with a shrug. 'Sure the girl must be dead for someone to talk to! Mick, boy, I was never one for criticizing religion, but God forgive me, that's not a natural life at all. I wouldn't stand it for a week. All those old hags!'

Mick, imagining the effect of Mrs Ryan on any well-organized convent, decided that God would probably not hold it too much against her, but he made up his mind to visit Nan. The convent was on one of the steep hills outside the city with a wide view of the valley from its front lawn. He was expecting a change but her appearance in the ugly convent parlour startled him. The frame of white linen and black veil gave her strongly marked features the unnatural relief of a fifteenth-century German portrait. And the twinkle of the big brown eyes convinced him of an idea that had been forming slowly in his mind through the years.

'Isn't it terrible I can't kiss you, Mick?' she said with a chuckle. 'I suppose I could really, but our old chaplain is a terror. He thinks I'm the New Nun. He's been hearing about her all his life, but I'm the first he's run across. Come into the garden where we can talk,' she added with an awed glance at the holy 71 pictures on the walls. 'This place would give you the creeps. I'm at them the whole time to get rid of that Sacred Heart. It's Bavarian, of course. They love it.'

Chattering on, she rustled ahead of him on to the lawn with her head bowed. He knew from the little flutter in her voice and manner that she was as pleased to see him as he was to see her. She led him to a garden seat behind a hedge that hid them from the convent and then grabbed in her enthusiastic way at his hand.

'Now, tell me all about you,' she said. 'I heard you were married to a very nice girl. One of the sisters went to school with her. She says she's a saint. Has she converted you yet?'

'Do I look as if she had?' he asked with a pale smile.

'No,' she replied with a chuckle. 'I'd know that agnostic look of yours anywhere. But you needn't think you'll escape me all the same.'

'You're a fierce pray-er,' he quoted, and she burst into a delighted laugh.

'It's true,' she said. 'I am. I'm a terror for holding on.'

'Really?' he asked mockingly. 'A girl that let two men slip in – what was it? a month?'

'Ah, that was different,' she said with sudden gravity. 'Then there were other things at stake. I suppose God came first.' Then she looked at him slyly out of the corner of her eye. 'Or do you think I'm only talking nonsense?'

'Don't you? What else is it?' he asked.

'I'm not really,' she said. 'Though I sometimes wonder myself how it all happened,' she added with a rueful shrug. 'And it's not that I'm not happy here. You know that?'

'Yes,' he said quietly. 'I've suspected that for quite a while.'

'My,' she said with a laugh, 'you *have* changed!'

He had not needed her to say that she was happy, nor did he need her to tell him why. He knew that the idea that had been forming in his mind for the last year or two was the true one, and that what had happened to her was not something unique and inexplicable. It was something that happened to others in different ways. Because of some inadequacy in themselves – poverty or physical weakness in men, poverty or ugliness in women – those with the gift of creation built for themselves a rich interior world; and when the inadequacy disappeared and the real world was spread before them with all its wealth 73 and beauty, they could not give their whole heart to it. Uncertain of their choice, they wavered between goals; were lonely in crowds, dissatisfied amid noise and laughter, unhappy even with those they loved best. The interior world called them back, and for some it was a case of having to return there or die.

He tried to explain this to her, feeling his own lack of persuasiveness and at the same time aware that she was watching him keenly and with amusement, almost as though she did not take him seriously. Perhaps she didn't, for which of us can feel, let alone describe, another's interior world? They sat there for close on an hour, listening to the convent bells calling one sister or another, and Mick refused to stay for tea. He knew convent tea parties, and had no wish to spoil the impression that their meeting had left on him.

'Pray for me,' he said with a smile as they shook hands.

'Do you think I ever stopped?' she replied with a mocking laugh, and he strode quickly down the shady steps to the lodge-gate in a strange mood of rejoicing, realizing that however the city might change, that old love-affair went on unbroken in a world where disgust or despair would never touch it, and would continue to do so till both of them were dead.

Song Without Words

Even if there were only two men left in the world and both of them saints they wouldn't be happy. One of them would be bound to try and improve the other. That is the nature of things.

I am not, of course, suggesting that either Brother Arnold or Brother Michael was a saint. In private life Brother Arnold was a postman, but as he had a great name as a cattle doctor they had put him in charge of the monastery cows. He had the sort of face you would expect to see advertising somebody's tobacco; a big, innocent, contented face with a pair of blue eyes that were always twinkling. According to the rule he was supposed to look sedate and go about in a composed and measured way, but he could not keep his eyes downcast for any length of time and wherever his eyes glanced they twinkled, and his hands slipped out of his long white sleeves and dropped some remark in sign language. Most of the monks were good at the deaf and dumb language; it was their way of getting round the rule of silence, and it was remarkable how much information they managed to pick up and pass on.

Now, one day it happened that Brother Arnold was looking for a bottle of castor oil and he remembered that he had lent it to Brother Michael, who was in charge of the stables. Brother Michael was a man he did not get on too well with; a dour, dull sort of man who kept to himself. He was a man of no great appearance, with a mournful wizened little face and a pair of weak red-rimmed eyes – for all the world the sort of man who, if you shaved off his beard, clapped a bowler hat on his head and a cigarette in his mouth, would need no other reference to get a job in a stable.

There was no sign of him about the stable yard, but this was only natural because he would not be wanted till the other monks returned from the fields, so Brother Arnold pushed in the stable door to look for the bottle himself. He did not see the bottle, but he saw something which made him wish he had not come. Brother Michael was hiding in one of the horse-boxes; standing against the partition with something hidden behind his back and wearing the look of a little boy who has been caught at the jam.

Something told Brother Arnold that at that moment

he was the most unwelcome man in the world. He grew red, waved his hand to indicate that he did not wish to be involved, and returned to his own quarters.

It came as a shock to him. It was plain enough that Brother Michael was up to some shady business, and Brother Arnold could not help wondering what it was. It was funny, he had noticed the same thing when he was in the world; it was always the quiet, sneaky fellows who were up to mischief. In chapel he looked at Brother Michael and got the impression that Brother Michael was looking at him, a furtive look to make sure he would not be noticed. Next day when they met in the yard he caught Brother Michael glancing at him and gave back a cold look and a nod.

The following day Brother Michael beckoned him to come over to the stables as though one of the horses was sick. Brother Arnold knew it wasn't that; he knew he was about to be given some sort of explanation and was curious to know what it would be. He was an inquisitive man; he knew it, and blamed himself a lot for it.

Brother Michael closed the door carefully after him and then leaned back against the jamb of the door with his legs crossed and his hands behind his 77 back, a foxy pose. Then he nodded in the direction of the horse-box where Brother Arnold had almost caught him in the act, and raised his brows inquiringly. Brother Arnold nodded gravely. It was not an occasion he was likely to forget. Then Brother Michael put his hand up his sleeve and held out a folded newspaper. Brother Arnold shrugged his shoulders as though to say the matter had nothing to do with him, but the other man nodded and continued to press the newspaper on him.

He opened it without any great curiosity, thinking it might be some local paper Brother Michael smuggled in for the sake of the news from home and was now offering as the explanation of his own furtive behaviour. He glanced at the name and then a great light broke on him. His whole face lit up as though an electric torch had been switched on behind, and finally he burst out laughing. He couldn't help himself. Brother Michael did not laugh but gave a dry little cackle which was as near as he ever got to laughing. The name of the paper was the *Irish Racing News*.

Now that the worst was over Brother Michael grew more relaxed. He pointed to a heading about the Curragh and then at himself. Brother Arnold shook his head, glancing at him expectantly as though he were hoping for another laugh. Brother Michael scratched his head for some indication of what he meant. He was a slow-witted man and had never been good at the sign talk. Then he picked up the sweeping brush and straddled it. He pulled up his skirts, stretched out his left hand holding the handle of the brush, and with his right began flogging the air behind him, a grim look on his leathery little face. Inquiringly he looked again and Brother Arnold nodded excitedly and put his thumbs up to show he understood. He saw now that the real reason Brother Michael had behaved so queerly was that he read racing papers on the sly and he did so because in private life he had been a jockey on the Curragh.

He was still laughing like mad, his blue eyes dancing, wishing only for an audience to tell it to, and then he suddenly remembered all the things he had thought about Brother Michael and bowed his head and beat his breast by way of asking pardon. Then he glanced at the paper again. A mischievous twinkle came into his eyes and he pointed the paper at himself. Brother Michael pointed back, a bit puzzled. Brother Arnold chuckled and stowed the paper up his sleeve. Then Brother Michael winked and gave the thumbs-up sign. In that slow cautious way of his he went down the stable and reached to the top of the wall where the roof sloped down on it. This, it seemed, was his hiding-hole. He took down several more papers and gave them to Brother Arnold.

For the rest of the day Brother Arnold was in the highest spirits. He winked and smiled at everyone till they all wondered what the joke was. He still pined for an audience. All that evening and long after he had retired to his cubicle he rubbed his hands and giggled with delight whenever he thought of it; it was like a window let into his loneliness; it gave him a warm, mellow feeling, as though his heart had expanded to embrace all humanity.

It was not until the following day that he had a chance of looking at the papers himself. He spread them on a rough desk under a feeble electric-light bulb high in the roof. It was four years since he had seen a paper of any sort, and then it was only a scrap of local newspaper which one of the carters had brought wrapped about a bit of bread and butter. But Brother Arnold had palmed it, hidden it in his desk, and studied it as if it were a bit of a lost Greek play. He had never known until then the modern appetite for words – printed words, regardless of their meaning. This was merely a County Council wrangle about the appointment of seven warble-fly inspectors, but by the time he was done with it he knew it by heart.

So he did not just glance at the racing papers as a man would in the train to pass the time. He nearly ate them. Blessed words like fragments of tunes coming to him out of a past life; paddocks and point-to-points and two-year-olds, and again he was in the middle of a racecourse crowd on a spring day with silver streamers of light floating down the sky like heavenly bunting. He had only to close his eyes and he could see the refreshment tent again with the golden light leaking like spilt honey through the rents in the canvas, and the girl he had been in love with sitting on an upturned lemonade box. 'Ah, Paddy,' she had said, 'sure there's bound to be racing in heaven!' She was fast, too fast for Brother Arnold, who was a steady-going fellow and had never got over the shock of discovering that all the time she had been running another man. But now all he could remember of her was her smile and the tone of her voice as she spoke the words which kept running through his head, and afterwards whenever his eyes met Brother Michael's he longed to give him a hearty slap on the back and say: 'Michael, boy, there's bound to be racing in heaven.' Then he grinned and Brother Michael, though he didn't hear the words or the tone of voice, without once losing his casual melancholy air, replied with a wall-faced flicker of the horny eyelid, a tick-tack man's signal, a real, expressionless, horsy look of complete understanding.

One day Brother Michael brought in a few papers. On one he pointed to the horses he had marked, on the other to the horses who had won. He showed no signs of his jubilation. He just winked, a leathery sort of wink, and Brother Arnold gaped as he saw the list of winners. It filled him with wonder and pride to think that when so many rich and clever people had lost, a simple little monk living hundreds of miles away could work it all out. The more he thought of it the more excited he grew. For one wild moment he felt it might be his duty to tell the Abbot, so that the monastery could have the full advantage of Brother Michael's intellect, but he realized that it wouldn't do. Even if Brother Michael could restore the whole abbey from top to bottom with his winnings, the ecclesiastical authorities would disapprove of it. But more than ever he felt the need of an audience.

He went to the door, reached up his long arm, and took down a loose stone from the wall above it. Brother Michael shook his head several times to indicate how impressed he was by Brother Arnold's ingenuity. Brother Arnold grinned. Then he took down a bottle and handed it to Brother Michael. The ex-jockey gave him a questioning look as though he were wondering if this wasn't cattle-medicine; his face did not change but he took out the cork and sniffed. Still his face did not change. All at once he went to the door, gave a quick glance up and a quick glance down and then raised the bottle to his lips. He reddened and coughed; it was good beer and he wasn't used to it. A shudder as of delight went through him and his little eyes grew moist as he watched Brother Arnold's throttle working on well-oiled hinges. The big man put the bottle back in its hiding-place and indicated by signs that Brother Michael could go there himself whenever he wanted a drink. Brother Michael shook his head doubtfully, but Brother Arnold nodded earnestly. His fingers moved like lightning while he explained how a farmer whose cow he had cured had it left in for him every week.

The two men were now fast friends. They no longer had any secrets from one another. Each knew the full extent of the other's little weakness and liked him the more for it. Though they couldn't speak to one another they sought out one another's company and whenever other things failed they merely smiled. Brother Arnold felt happier than he had felt for years. Brother Michael's successes made him want to try his hand, and whenever Brother Michael gave him a racing paper with his own selections marked, Brother Arnold gave it back with his, and they waited impatiently till the results turned up three or four days late. It was also a new lease of life to Brother Michael, for what comfort is it to a man if he has all the winners when not a soul in the world can ever know whether he has or not. He felt now that if only he could have a bob each way on a horse he would ask no more of life.

It was Brother Arnold, the more resourceful of the pair, who solved that difficulty. He made out dockets, each valued for so many Hail Marys, and the loser had to pay up in prayers for the other man's intention. It was an ingenious scheme and it worked admirably. At first Brother Arnold had a run of luck. But it wasn't for nothing that Brother Michael had

had the experience; he was too tough to make a fool of himself even over a few Hail Marys, and everything he did was carefully planned. Brother Arnold began by imitating him, but the moment he struck it lucky he began to gamble wildly. Brother Michael had often seen it happen on the Curragh and remembered the fate of those it had happened to. Men he had known with big houses and cars were now cadging drinks in the streets of Dublin. It struck him that God had been very good to Brother Arnold in calling him to a monastic life where he could do no harm to himself or to his family.

And this, by the way, was quite uncalled for, because in the world Brother Arnold's only weakness had been for a bottle of stout and the only trouble he had ever caused his family was the discomfort of having to live with a man so good and gentle, but Brother Michael was rather given to a distrust of human nature, the sort of man who goes looking for a moral in everything even when there is no moral in it. He tried to make Brother Arnold take an interest in the scientific side of betting but the man seemed to treat it all as a great joke. A flighty sort of fellow! He bet more and more wildly with that foolish good-natured grin on his face, and after a while Brother 85

Michael found himself being owed a deuce of a lot of prayers, which his literal mind insisted on translating into big houses and cars. He didn't like that either. It gave him scruples of conscience and finally turned him against betting altogether. He tried to get Brother Arnold to drop it, but as became an inventor, Brother Arnold only looked hurt and indignant, like a child who has been told to stop his play. Brother Michael had that weakness on his conscience too. It suggested that he was getting far too attached to Brother Arnold, as in fact he was. It would have been very difficult not to. There was something warm and friendly about the man which you couldn't help liking.

Then one day he went in to Brother Arnold and found him with a pack of cards in his hand. They were a very old pack which had more than served their time in some farmhouse, but Brother Arnold was looking at them in rapture. The very sight of them gave Brother Michael a turn. Brother Arnold made the gesture of dealing, half playfully, and the other shook his head sternly. Brother Arnold blushed and bit his lip but he persisted, seriously enough now. All the doubts Brother Michael had been having for weeks turned to conviction. This was the primrose path with a vengeance, one thing leading to another. Brother Arnold grinned and shuffled the deck; Brother Michael, biding his time, cut for deal and Brother Arnold won. He dealt two hands of five and showed the five of hearts as trump. He wanted to play twenty-five. Still waiting for a sign, Brother Michael looked at his own hand. His face grew grimmer. It was not the sort of sign he had expected but it was a sign all the same; four hearts in a bunch; the ace, jack, two other trumps, and the three of spades. An unbeatable hand. Was that luck? Was that coincidence, or was it the Adversary himself, taking a hand and trying to draw him deeper in the mire.

He liked to find a moral in things, and the moral in this was plain, though it went to his heart to admit it. He was a lonesome, melancholy man and the horses had meant a lot to him in his bad spells. At times it had seemed as if they were the only thing that kept him sane. How could he face twenty, perhaps thirty, years more of life, never knowing what horses were running or what jockeys were up – Derby Day, Punchestown, Leopardstown, and the Curragh all going by while he knew no more of them than if he were already dead?

'O Lord,' he thought bitterly, 'a man gives up the whole world for You, his chance of a wife and kids, his home and his family, his friends and his job, and goes off to a bare mountain where he can't even tell his troubles to the man alongside him; and still he keeps something back, some little thing to remind him of what he gave up. With me 'twas the horses and with this man 'twas the sup of beer, and I dare say there are fellows inside who have a bit of a girl's hair hidden somewhere they can go and look at it now and again. I suppose we all have our little hiding-hole if the truth was known, but as small as it is, the whole world is in it, and bit by bit it grows on us again till the day You find us out.'

Brother Arnold was waiting for him to play. He sighed and put his hand on the desk. Brother Arnold looked at it and at him. Brother Michael idly took away the spade and added the heart and still Brother Arnold couldn't see. Then Brother Michael shook his head and pointed to the floor. Brother Arnold bit his lip again as though he were on the point of crying, then threw down his own hand and walked to the other end of the cow-house. Brother Michael left him so for a few moments. He could see the struggle going on in the man, could almost hear the Devil whisper in his ear that he (Brother Michael) was only an old woman – Brother Michael had heard that before; that life was long and a man might as well be dead and buried as not have some little innocent amusement – the sort of plausible whisper that put many a man on the gridiron. He knew, however hard it was now, that Brother Arnold would be grateful to him in the other world. 'Brother Michael,' he would say, 'I don't know what I'd ever have done without your example.'

Then Brother Michael went up and touched him gently on the shoulder. He pointed to the bottle, the racing paper, and the cards. Brother Arnold fluttered his hands despairingly but he nodded. They gathered them up between them, the cards, the bottle, and the papers, hid them under their habits to avoid all occasion of scandal, and went off to confess their guilt to the Prior.

For complete information about books available from Penguin and how to order them, please write to us at the appropriate address below. Please note that for copyright reasons the selection of books varies from country to country.

IN THE UNITED KINGDOM: Please write to *Dept. JC, Penguin Books Ltd, FREEPOST, West Drayton, Middlesex UB7 0BR.*
If you have any difficulty in obtaining a title, please send your order with the correct money, plus ten per cent for postage and packaging, to *PO Box No. 11, West Drayton, Middlesex UB7 0BR.*

IN THE UNITED STATES: Please write to *Consumer Sales, Penguin USA, P.O. Box 999, Dept. 17109, Bergenfield, New Jersey 07621-0120.* VISA and MasterCard holders call 1-800-253-6476 to order all Penguin titles.

IN CANADA: Please write to *Penguin Books Canada Ltd, 10 Alcorn Avenue, Suite 300, Toronto, Ontario M4V 3B2.*

IN AUSTRALIA: Please write to *Penguin Books Australia Ltd, P.O. Box 257, Ringwood, Victoria 3134.*

IN NEW ZEALAND: Please write to *Penguin Books (NZ) Ltd, Private Bag 102902, North Shore Mail Centre, Auckland 10.*

IN INDIA: Please write to *Penguin Books India Pvt Ltd, 706 Eros Apartments, 56 Nehru Place, New Delhi 110 019.*

IN THE NETHERLANDS: Please write to *Penguin Books Netherlands bv, Postbus 3507, NL-1001 AH Amsterdam.*

IN GERMANY: Please write to *Penguin Books Deutschland GmbH, Metzlerstrasse 26, 60594 Frankfurt am Main.*

IN SPAIN: Please write to *Penguin Books S. A., Bravo Murillo 19, 1o B, 28015 Madrid.*

IN ITALY: Please write to *Penguin Italia s.r.l., Via Felice Casati 20, I-20124 Milano.*

IN FRANCE: Please write to *Penguin France S. A., 17 rue Lejeune, F-31000 Toulouse.*

IN JAPAN: Please write to *Penguin Books Japan, Ishikiribashi Building, 2-5-4, Suido, Bunkyo-ku, Tokyo 112.*

IN GREECE: Please write to *Penguin Hellas Ltd, Dimocritou 3, GR-106 71 Athens.*

IN SOUTH AFRICA: Please write to *Longman Penguin Southern Africa (Pty) Ltd, Private Bag X08, Bertsham 2013.*